Faye's Fortune

by
Emmy Tidning

Applied Divination
Redmond

Faye's Fortune
Copyright © 2021 Emmy Tidning
ISBN 978-1-7356170-6-0

Published by Applied Divination
Edited by Emily Paper
Formatted for print by Applied Divination

This book is a work of fiction. If any part of Faye's Fortune resembles the life of a known person, living or dead, then they are and were very lucky, indeed.

First printing edition 2021
Applied Divination
www.applieddivination.com

CHAPTER ONE

Faith hauled a thirty-pound box of gemstones down the sidewalk, pleased about her find at the estate sale across the street. She felt bad that she'd never introduced herself to the neighbor before they died, but the collection of gems seemed to speak magic from beyond the grave. She had to have them for her shop, so she'd used her last five bucks to buy them.

I guess I won't be buying coffee today, Faith said to herself.

The heavy box stifled her ability to see the sidewalk, so every step was an estimate, at best. She knew there were some overgrown plants somewhere along the way. She'd stumbled over them plenty of times.

"But I won't stumble today," she promised herself out loud.

An electric vehicle pulled up to the curb beside her, surprising her with its silent approach. At that moment her foot hit a twig and her body pitched forward. The box of crystals seemed to launch out of her arms as though in slow motion.

"Nope, wrong. Definitely will stumble today," she sputtered as her body splayed out on the pavement. A myriad of gemstones, from golden topaz to purple amethyst, scattered around her.

"Oh shit," a deep voice said, "did I do that? My car is too quiet."

From her new spot on the ground, Faith heard the car door slam and sensed the driver's strong legs moving in her direction.

"Don't worry about it," she desperately scrambled up to her knees to try and look less like a inebriated spider. "It wasn't you; it was this pretty fairy garden growing over the sidewalk-"

She dusted pavement off her thighs, "-as well as my own clumsiness."

A steady palm reached down to her eye level, and immediately she noticed a smooth, deep heart line stretching across it. This person was a lover, not a fighter. Smaller lines etched across his sturdy appendage. He was also a hard worker.

"Thank you," she took his hand, and a small jolt of electricity shook them both.

Faith giggled, still quite humiliated from the fall, and she rose unsteadily rose to her feet. Finally, she changed her view from that of the pavement toward her rescuer.

The warm hand was attached to a muscular arm, which itself was joined to a toned body, down to those strong legs and, finally, upward to an extremely cute face.

Faith felt something flutter in her belly.

She shoved the feeling into her metaphorical mind storage unit for *fluffy gutter nonsense I'm far too busy to think about.*

"Let me help you pick these up," the man said to her, bending over to grab some fallen stones. Immediately the butterflies came back. His voice was soft and sensual, like a smooth-talking radio host.

She made a mental note to listen to the radio more often.

"It's really okay," Faith insisted, "I always hit that same spot on the sidewalk."

He looked into her eyes and being consumed by his irises felt like cartwheeling through fields of gold. She tried desperately to pull her attention away from the soul-melting pools of hazel splendor, but-

What the hell is wrong with me? She thought to herself.

She waved her hand in the general vicinity of the plants which had so ungraciously tripped her in front of this stunning being, but she also sent a mental thank-you to them for the adventure.

He ended the staring contest first, and the moment was over. Faith again tried to adjust her position to look slightly less like a previously upended turtle, and more like a gymnast bouncing back from a strategic flip.

The guy pushed away some of the overgrown vines. "This is pretty bad. The clematis have grown under the sidewalk and pushed parts of it up."

He spoke about clematis as though his lilting words were a poem that could fix it. Faith fawned.

"I'll get my guys to check it out. Here, let me help you get all these."

"Guys? These?" Faith was lost in a head full of butterflies.

He pointed at the ground, and she remembered the box of a hundred crystals she'd bought not five minutes before, now littering the sidewalk in all their shiny translucent splendor.

The man bent down and started picking up gemstones, tucking his dark auburn hair behind his ear.

Faith wondered if the carpet matched the drapes.

She gasped at herself, and he raised an eyebrow up at her.

This is not who I am, she thought, and shook herself back into reality.

"Thanks, it really is okay," she breathed, scrambling to find the box and relocate her thoughts from nonsense to reality. She knelt down and crawled after some obsidian spheres which had rolled the furthest away.

"It was my own fault," she said, "I knew those vines were there, I walk this way every day."

"JJ knew they were there, too," said a small, teasing voice from the other side of the hedge.

Faith couldn't see anyone from her spot on the ground.

"Hi Gran," the man – presumably, JJ – stood and smiled. "I actually came over to see if I could fix this for you today."

To Faith, he said, "this is my Grandmother's house."

"Hello, dear" a familiar lady peeked her head around the corner of the hedge. Faith had seen her many times, sitting on her porch with the now-deceased neighbor, but she'd never introduced herself.

"Hi," she tried to scramble to her feet. "I'm sorry for your loss. I live in that ugly apartment townhouse across the street."

The three of them looked at the townhouse and frowned. It was very unsightly compared to this woman's cute cottage, even with the overgrown clematis everywhere.

The lady smiled, "I know you do, dear. Sorry about the sidewalk. JJ, help the poor girl with her crystals."

"Yes ma'am," he reached down to retrieve a carnelian from the flower bed. Faith watched him bend over and then she kept watching.

"Hey, this one is really pretty," he eyed the stone.

Faith shook herself out of her stupor again. With pride, she beamed, "I'm going to display them in my shop! I got them from the estate sale next door, all for just five bucks!"

Which is good, because Charlotte would kill me if I spent any more money we don't have.

Faith's cheeks tickled her, and she apologized again to the elderly woman for her loss. She was pleased that she could afford them, though.

The elderly woman smiled, "Frannie was such an avid collector of gems. I'm glad they'll go to someone who appreciates them."

"Gran collects rocks too," JJ carefully placed the carnelian into the cardboard box, like a new father settling a newborn baby into a bassinet.

Faith melted.

"They're not rocks," his gran scorned him.

Faith slapped herself in the face again, mentally.

He asked, "What kind of shop do you have?"

At this question, Faith felt her defenses instinctively take over. As cute as he was, she did not want another mansplainer laughing at her business. She was -*usually*, she reminded herself- quite skilled at her craft, but these brawny men always mocked her first, then were only ever stunned at her insights later.

"It's a spiritual occult shop," she said carefully. More boldly, she stated "I'm a fortune teller."

"Oh!" the man smiled, "Faye's Fortunes? The one over there on the corner?"

She nodded with skepticism.

"My construction team put the decorative glass stones into the sidewalk. I'm the best sidewalk game in town. My gran is into that witchy stuff, too."

The little old lady swatted at him, "it's not 'witchy stuff' you silly layman."

Faith giggled and blushed again, embarrassed that she'd thought he would mock her, and loving the banter between him and his grandmother.

"I love our sidewalk," she said, "thanks to your team for doing that. They're exactly how we wanted our entrance to look and the glass stones are very welcoming."

Now if only the shop had more customers to welcome, she felt her conscience nagging at her.

"We were super proud of that sidewalk," he grinned. "Totally beats installing boring concrete any day."

"I'm sure."

They smiled at each other for a long moment, then seemingly at the same time each of them realized his grandmother was still watching them. They turned in opposite directions and continued to pick up the gemstones and crystals.

"Hi Sure, I'm Jasper," he said a minute later.

"Huh," Faith snapped out of a brief daydream where she was making out with him on a bed of clematis and carnelian.

He blew out a shy laugh and opened his mouth to speak, and that's when she understood his joke.

"Oh! I get it. Because I said, 'I'm sure.' Ha ha, duh." *Okay stop talking now,* she reproached herself. Then she took a breath and continued, "I'm Faith. Or Faye, for short."

His eyebrow curled. "Faith is already shor-"

"I know, I know" she shrugged, retrieving a white quartz from a crack in the sidewalk, "but Faye is a better name for a psychic. Faith is a little too ingénue for that."

He seemed to think about this for a split second, contemplating a Tiger's Eye he'd found near the curb. "I get that. My real name is Jasper, like the stone. It's sort of strange for a sidewalk concrete paver."

He tilted his eyes away as though he were also embarrassed. Faith's chest warmed up a few degrees.

"I like Jasper! The stone and the name," she insisted, then added quickly, "I like JJ too."

"JJ is short for Jasper Jacob," the elderly woman said, "but I never liked the name Jacob. It's too harsh for my sweet boy."

"Gran! She doesn't need to know my life story or your opinions," Jasper huffed in feigned frustration.

Faye giggled again and felt her cheeks burn even deeper. She scrambled to grab another handful of stones from the pavement behind her.

Jasper seemed to do the same, finding colorful stones in the bushes near the fairy garden.

Faye stood, and Jasper picked the box up to hand to her. He waited until she had a good strong grip on it before letting it go.

"There's a lot of rocks in there," he said stupidly, then shook his head slightly as if admonishing himself.

Faith laughed.

The Tiger's Eye was still in his hand. He admired it again before gently setting it in the box.

"Yeah, this was a great haul," Faye steadied the heavy box in one arm and picked the Tiger's eye stone back out. "You can keep this one if you'd like. It matches your eyes."

She held the rock up beside his face and stared deeply at it, then looked at him. He looked right through it at her.

Her belly fluttered again.

He looked away and held up a hand "Nah, it's okay. Gran has plenty of these."

"I insist. I only wish I had a jasper gemstone, too." She fumbled awkwardly through the box hoping jasper might appear, as though she hadn't already analyzed every stone before scooping up the inventory. "I know this stuff sounds silly, but-"

"-It doesn't," he insisted, not even knowing what she was about to say.

"Tiger's Eye is believed to invoke courage. It will ground you during times of great stress."

"Oh?"

He smiled and took the stone from her, brushing his fingers against hers and sending shivers up her arm. He stared into it and started saying, "Courage would be great because-"

"Jacob!" an exasperated cry reverberated from somewhere behind Faith. "I've been looking all over for you for five whole minutes!"

Faith took a step back and turned to see a stunningly gorgeous goddess approach from the street corner. Her beauty seemed to command the attention of the world just by its mere existence, although her shriek had also commanded a fair bit of that attention as well. Some Main street shoppers stopped to stare. In her hands were bags Faith recognized from the village boutiques.

"Kelsey. I'm sorry," Jasper whispered an apology from behind Faith, and she wondered if it was to herself or the goddess. He continued, "you knew I was at Gran's though. There was a small accident."

Faith tried to apologize for him, "Jasper was just helping me with-"

"Jacob," Kelsey corrected Faith's use of his name, "Jasper is a dumb name."

"Right, sure, sorry. I spilled my gemstones and he-"

"I've been carrying these heavy bags waiting for you," Kelsey whimpered, dropping the bags like they weighed a thousand pounds.

Jasper placed the Tiger's Eye back into Faith's box and grabbed his phone out of his pocket. He tapped a few buttons and the front of his car opened to reveal storage space.

Faith watched as he dashed to Kelsey's side to grab the bags, which he then loaded smoothly into the car. The bags seemed like nothing.

"I need to get out of here, it's getting so warm." Kelsey laid a tired hand across her forehead.

It's nine a.m. and like twenty degrees, Faith thought to herself. Then, *shut up, me.*

"Of course, babe. There's water in the car."

"I want lemonade," Kelsey grumbled, pawing for the car door handle in frustration.

From behind the hood, Jasper shrugged and mouthed an 'I'm sorry,' either to Faith or his Grandmother, it was hard to tell whom. Perhaps both.

Faith smiled, held up the Tiger's Eye, and tossed it in his direction. "Please take it," she insisted, "for your kindness today."

He whispered a thank-you, and for a moment it felt as if he were staring into her soul.

She watched him tuck the small stone into his breast pocket without taking his gaze away, and he patted his chest to secure it. She wondered how warm his body was at that spot so close to his heart.

She shook herself and double-checked that his - *girlfriend? Wife? Soon-to-be ex? Please be a soon-to-be ex —* didn't see her blush.

"Bye Gran," Jasper said, and Faith remembered that his Grandmother was standing right behind her. No wonder he was staring!

Faith turned and nodded her own goodbye to the lady, then scrambled out of there before her flushed cheeks could embarrass her any further.

The lady laughed, "you will visit again, dear."

Faith could have sworn it was stated as an auspicious fact, not a casual farewell.

CHAPTER TWO

Faith sat in front of the makeup mirror, staring at her still flushed cheeks.

"You don't need any blush for work today, do you, babe?" Charlotte pulled at a strand of Faith's hair and twisted a green feather into it.

If it was possible to blush further, she did. "I met a nice, cute guy."

Charlotte made a wide, excited face in the mirror. she reached for a hairbrush, eyeing Faith and nonverbally pleading for more information.

"It's nothing," said Faith, "Really. He helped me pick up the crystals I spilled this morning. Said his name was Jasper."

"Ohhhh, like the mysterious gemstone. You got his name, too? You move fast! What's his number?" Charlotte's eyebrow shot up and she beamed.

"I mean, we had some time to chat while we picked up the stones. I told him I own this shop. His bricklaying team did our walkway out front!"

"Ooo, a skilled bricklayer! Sexy! I wonder what else he lays well." Charlotte winked.

Faith's cheeks burned. "It doesn't matter. He has a girlfriend and she's hot."

"You're hotter," said Charlotte.

"You didn't see her, you nut."

"I don't need to. I have a feeling."

"A *psychic* feeling?" Faith snickered.

Charlotte yanked her hair. "You're the psychic in this joint, but I'm sure your skills were bound to wear off on me eventually. Now, draw us a tarot card while I work on your feathers."

Faith pulled a Tarot deck from the makeup drawer and shuffled, watching in the mirror as Charlotte carefully placed more feathers in her hair. "Do you think these are necessary?"

"It gives me something to do in the morning before we open. Plus," added Charlotte, "without them you look like a normal, everyday Faith Sybertz. With them, you become Faye Sybella, the famous psychic from Fallstaff, Missouri."

"I wouldn't say I'm famous in this town, Charlie."

"Does a cute sidewalk construction guy know who you are?"

"Well yes, but-"

"Then you're famous! Own it! We're going to do big things in this town, babe. Just wait."

"From your mouth to Goddess's ears," Faith cut the deck and placed it back down in the drawer. "but first we need more people and money through the door. I'm about to be evicted."

"Draw a card. Maybe sales will improve today," Charlotte paused to watch Faith's daily prediction, a feather poking out from behind her teeth.

"Reversed Judgment," Faith sighed, holding up the card. "Not today."

Charlotte frowned. "Nah, you're reading it wrong. It's probably just a warning not to doubt ourselves."

Faith set the card back on top of the others. "For a non-psychic you're pretty good at reading Tarot cards."

Charlotte shrugged. "One day I may have to stop doing Reiki massages and instead step in as a psychic-in-residence. Especially if you're out gallivanting in the streets with muscle-bound concrete pavers. All done."

Faith smirked but took a moment to admire herself in the mirror. The green and blue feathers woven throughout her hair were indeed transformational. With her fresh coat of blue and green eyeshadow, she looked mysterious, ominous, and all-knowing.

"Faye Sybella, famous psychic," she whispered to herself as though she were a stranger gawking at a celebrity.

"That's the spirit, Faye-faye. Now, let's go get some customers."

The mood faltered a little. The reverse judgement card stared up at them both, reminding Faith that business was terrible.

She slammed the drawer shut.

CHAPTER THREE

As the Reversed Judgment card had predicted, there wasn't much business that morning. Charlotte had one weekly Reiki appointment with a lovely old woman who drove in from Jefferson City, but because of her commute she'd wanted the fee cut to twenty dollars from forty. Charlotte had agreed to the discount just to have a regular customer.

Faye had no clients. Main street was devoid of shoppers, and school was in session so there weren't any teenagers popping in for a psychic prediction to pass the time.

"Maybe we could offer hair or makeup services too," Faith suggested as Charlotte waved goodbye to her customer and closed the shop door.

"We're not cosmetologists, we're spiritual practitioners," Charlotte asserted with the hint of a sigh. She made it look like she was adjusting a set of string lights in the front window, but Faith knew she was checking the street outside for any person at all.

"I'm starting to wonder if maybe the universe is looking for more practical goals out of us." Faith walked to the back office and stuck the customer's twenty-dollar bill in the till. She frowned at its lack of other contents, then closed the drawer and leaned against the doorway. "Maybe the reversed judgment card was telling us that this isn't our calling."

"Bull. This is what we've wanted and trained for our entire lives." Charlotte held her hands up and spun around the reception area, forcing Faye to behold and admire their work.

Beautiful velvet curtains hung on the walls and windows, plush and pillowy seats filled the floor, crystals and occult divination items adorned every shelf, and among them were random piles of fortune telling books, cards, and boxes of divinatory enchantment. It was messy but magical.

Charlotte continued, "we finally own our shop. Your name is Faith and you need to have some faith now. This *is* our calling and the customers *will* come."

"How do you know?"

Charlotte approached and held her palms up toward Faith's face, not touching her but holding them close enough that Faith could feel the heat radiating from her hands. It was like magic Reiki energy for her soul.

"I can sense success in you," Charlotte stated.

Faith had doubts, but her friend's confidence was inviting and uplifting. She couldn't help but lean in for a hug.

"Careful now, your feathers will stab my eyes out, Madam Sybella," Charlotte laughed.

The door chimed, and a gust of chilly Spring air blew into the room.

"A customer," Charlotte whispered excitedly. "I'll go clean up my massage room."

"I'll find out what they want," Faith muttered.

Charlotte raised an eyebrow. "Not with that scowl and attitude you won't," she quietly asserted. "Confidence, mystery, and poise. You are Faye Sybella, famed mystic of central Missouri."

"Ooo, now it's not just Fallstaff, it's the entire center of the state," Faith teased.

"There's no other psychic in central Missouri but you," Charlotte winked, and she feigned drifting on a cloud toward her massage room. To the client, Faye heard Charlotte purr "Madam Sybella will be right with you."

Faith backed up into the office, adjusted her flowing blouse, and primped her feathers until they felt like they were floating on their own. As graciously as possible, she glided toward the front of the reception area like wind caught in a sail.

She opened her mouth to speak and stopped dead in her tracks.

Before her stood the stunning girlfriend from earlier that morning, Kelsey.

Faith caught her breath and smiled, "Why hello, how are you?"

Kelsey's gaze wandered around the items in the room, and she raised a curious but critical eyebrow. "Great. I want one of those Tarot readings." She grinned, and as an afterthought she added, "you know, for a laugh."

Tarot is serious business, not a laugh, Faith wanted to say, but didn't. She got clients like this all the time and had learned long ago that it was better to entertain them and get paid, than to school them and get bad reviews for the shop.

"Of course," Faith grinned through her teeth, "After a busy morning of shopping and waiting for your lover, it's time to relax with Madam Sybella."

Kelsey's jaw could have mopped the floor. "How'd you know I had to wait for my boyfriend?!"

Now it was Faith's turn to raise an eyebrow. Then it dawned on her that Kelsey had no idea she was the girl Jasper had assisted earlier that morning. Perhaps her blue eyeshadow and feathered hair had disguised what hours ago was merely a klutz with a box of rocks.

That, or the woman hadn't even noticed there was another person present that morning at all.

"Faye Sybella knows everything," she ventured carefully. "Please proceed into my reading room and rest your weary legs. I'll be right with you."

As Kelsey moved into the small room off the reception area, Faith briefly dropped the confident air and tripled checked her hair and makeup in a mirror again. She did not want to blow her cover or screw this up.

"You look great, Faye" Charlotte whispered from behind her, smiling coyly from the doorway to her treatment room, "now go get me some money!"

CHAPTER FOUR

When the shop was first opened, Faith was quite confident she'd put together her psychic reading room in a self-explanatory way. A wall of tulle curtains surrounded her dark red mystic's armchair, and in front of it a crystal ball, some gemstones, her Runes, and her Tarot cards lay waiting for the psychic to sit before them. Across the table from that was a very welcoming guest chair, with easy, welcoming access for customers to sit upon. It was the far more convenient chair, being perfectly placed between the door and window, whereas Faith's seat required extra work to get into.

But Kelsey had chosen the mystic's chair, and when Faith entered the room, she found the woman fingering the crystal ball as though it were her own.

Faith frowned and wondered if she should correct her, or just suck it up. She had to pull herself together to stay in character.

"I see you have opted for my chair. That tells me a lot about who you are as a person," she stated. It was a dig, but one that was so subtle she doubted Kelsey would understand it.

"I just don't want any head games," Kelsey eyed her and played with a tower of quartz, "I don't know what you can do or see from here."

"I see all from anywhere," Faye said and tried to hide her self-doubt. Although this was her room and her element, the lack of funds and customers had her questioning her abilities lately. Theoretically, it shouldn't matter what seat she did a reading from, but with business the way it was, who knew?

She sat in the guest chair and chose to use this rare opportunity to double-check that everything looked good and magical from the seat of her customers.

It did, and she started to regain some of her lost confidence.

"Do you want your ball?" Kelsey reached to move the crystal globe.

"No," Faith stammered, trying to stop Kelsey from touching it any more than she already had. The ball was precarious, and if it rolled off the table it could shatter into pieces.

Faith calmed herself and added, "I don't need an orb to see all."

Kelsey sat back and eyed her.

Faith reached for a Tarot deck and started shuffling. "So, what can I help you with? What questions do you have?"

"Shouldn't you already know all this, psychic?" Kelsey smirked, looking at her nails. Faith watched her fiddle with a freshly painted set of acrylics.

She was testing her, and Faith wondered why. Was this an actual, real-life two-dimensional human - one with zero knowledge about divination and a testy personality, or was Kelsey going through something much deeper and taking it out on whomever she could find?

Faith considered her options. If Kelsey was, in fact, just a mean-girl type who thought fortune telling was nonsense, she probably would not have come in the store. Not alone, anyway. She would bring a group of friends so they could mock Faye Sybella together.

No, something deeper was up, and Faye might have to dig to get at it.

"I can see you are suffering," Faith said carefully, then cautiously added, "in your romantic life."

Kelsey's eyes lit up and she sat a little straighter. "You see that?"

I saw it this morning. If you cared at all about anyone but yourself you would have noticed me, Faith said to herself.

She instantly regretted the thought. She would have to be far less judgmental if she ever wanted repeat business.

Reverse this judgment, her conscience told her.

Reversed judgment. Maybe not judging her clients was the warning the Reversed Judgement Tarot card was trying to give her that morning.

She closed her eyes tight, which made Faye appear to be deep in focus, but helped Faith get over herself and consider how best to continue with the reading.

"Madam Sybella sees all," she opened her eyes.

Kelsey grabbed the cards out of her hands, shaking Faye's train of thought.

"I can't wait any longer, What's your prediction," Kelsey asked. She started laying out Tarot cards in front of herself.

The Tower card appeared, followed by the three of swords.

Ominous and terrible ends, heartbreak. There was no good news there.

"I see a divorce," Faye said.

Kelsey looked like she was about to rebut the statement. Although most people had a divorce somewhere in their lives, sometimes they were so caught up in their own heads, they would say something like 'I'm not married,' or 'that's not happening' before they stopped to consider all the possibilities.

"-and an affair," Faye added quickly.

Kelsey held a hand to her mouth, "You see an affair?"

Faye wondered if she wanted more details or was just questioning the card. "An affair or possibly a love triangle," she said, "but either way it won't end well."

Kelsey laughed. "No, I know there's an affair. I feel it. I'm just shocked that you can see all that."

It was Faye's turn to let her jaw drop a little. Her shoulders fell temporarily, and she had to remind herself that Kelsey had no idea who she was.

Was Jasper cheating on Kelsey? Was she cheating on him? Was Faye the third wheel in this weird affair love triangle?

Faye repeated the morning's events in her head. Jasper had seemed like such a nice guy. He did not seem like the type to have a wild affair, although he was a little flirty with Faith. But nothing had happened with her except for her own brain making up fantasy makeout sessions with him.

Faith wanted to find out what was going on, for her own edification and peace of mind. But she knew she'd be treading dangerous waters if she purposefully broke up the couple before their time.

She decided to try a different way to get to the bottom of what was happening.

For Kelsey, she convinced herself, *because she's my customer.*

"I see a gemstone," Faye said, "laid in fresh concrete."

Kelsey glared at her for a second. "What the hell does that mean?"

"A precious gemstone forged from volcanic ash. A Jasper stone."

"Oh!" Kelsey sat up, delighted. "That's my boyfriend! And the concrete is probably his lame sidewalks!"

"Yes, yes," Faye said, and laid down another card. The reversed King of cups. "I see his heart is in two places."

Faith wondered again if he was the one who was cheating. Who was this reading for?

Kelsey said, "He's got a stupid zoo job so he never has any time for me. But I'm not breaking up with him, if that's what that building card means," Kelsey waved at the Tower card on the table.

"Your boyfriend works at a zoo?" Faye was confused. He said he was a bricklayer, and Kelsey had confirmed it earlier.

"He volunteers cleaning up after seals or whatever on weekends. It's disgusting and I want him to quit it. What do the cards say?"

Faye laid down another card. The reversed Lovers. Sometimes it meant a breakup, but other times it meant that one's head and heart were not matching up. She wondered if it represented Kelsey's head and heart, or Jasper's, or her own.

"The cards think you will break up with your boyfriend."

"Ha! Not anytime soon," laughed Kelsey, "he's got a great condo in Jefferson City and if I play my cards right, I can move right in and get the hell out of this yokel town."

Faith considered Kelsey for a moment. She *was* a mean girl after all. A villain with no motivations except to inflict pain on others for her own success. A narcissist of the highest degree. Faith had never met an actual two-dimensional human being before.

That, or maybe Jasper was cheating on her and Faye had unwittingly just notified Kelsey of that fact. Maybe Kelsey deserved to break out of this town and try something new.

Faye stared into the crystal ball, not knowing what to say next. She thought hard about what was happening. Her interaction with Jasper this morning was irrelevant to Kelsey, but what if Kelsey will hurt him? But also, what if he is hurting *her*? Should she say something to him? What type of client confidentiality agreement does a street fortune teller have with the people she reads for?

Kelsey interrupted Faye's thoughts and ogled the ball. "What? What is happening? Are you seeing something? What is it?"

Faith realized she'd been staring at the ball far too long. She shook herself out of her stupor.

"Yes, yes, I see something," she lied.

"What is it?" Kelsey's face opened brightly in wonderment.

"Money and power," Faye tested.

"For me?! Oh my gosh, yay! I'm moving on up to Jefferson City!"

"Yes," Faye said, "maybe. That part is unclear. Only time will divine from where your fortunes derive."

Kelsey seemed pleased with this and stood to leave, fishing her long acrylics into a too-small handbag. She pulled out a folded ten-dollar bill and tossed it on the table.

"Thanks Sybil or whatever," she beamed.

It's Madam Sybella, thought Faith. *Or Faye is fine. Also, a reading is twenty-five bucks, but okay. Just get out of my store.*

"I'll tell my friends about you," Kelsey bounced through the reception room and out the shop door. The bells on the door sang as she left.

Charlotte stood in the reception area and stared after her, clearly confused as to why she wasn't even acknowledged on Kelsey's way by.

"Count your blessings," said Faith, reading her mind and handing her the ten-dollar bill.

Charlotte frowned at the underpayment but walked back to the till. "It's something," she said as she put it in the drawer.

"Yeah, it's something," Faith agreed.

But what?

CHAPTER FIVE

Charlotte's cheap Reiki client and Kelsey turned out to be the shop's only business of the day. Charlotte and Faith spent the afternoon puttering around the business, shifting small items around as though that would invite more clients, and posting pics on their store social media accounts, in the hopes that some grassroots marketing might help.

While dusting off a jar of rusty nails Faith wondered aloud, "There is a sort of client-fortune-teller privilege, don't you think?"

"Hmm?" Charlotte looked up from an unopened crate of Tarot cards on the floor. "No, I don't think there is anything like that at all."

Charlotte's attention moved from the box of Tarot cards to the one with estate gemstones that Faith had bought earlier that day. She started looking through them, and delicately placed a few on the retail shelves, turning them to catch their shiniest sides in the light. "I could sell these as part of my Reiki practice. I think we could get five bucks each for these, and maybe we could turn a bit of a profit that way."

"Aw, I wanted those for decoration only," whined Faith, but she admitted to herself that they neither had the money for decor nor the space to display them all.

"I suppose you're right," she said. "They're better off finding new homes that will appreciate them. I don't know what I'll do about Jasper."

Charlotte pushed some stones around in the box, "I don't think there's a lot of jasper in here. Maybe this one," she held up a shimmering stone to the light, "but I actually think it's polished agate."

"Hmm," Faith stared absentmindedly out the shop window.

"Oh," Charlotte placed the agate on a low shelf. "You weren't talking about Jasper *stones*, were you? You have a mad crush on this guy."

"It's not a crush," Faith insisted. "I'm just wondering about him now that I know his relationship is going to bust up into a million pieces pretty soon."

"And you want to be the one to rush in and pick up the mess, don't you? I don't blame you. He sounds positively divine."

Faith adjusted a few curtains. "What do you mean he sounds divine?"

"You've been talking about him all day!"

"I have?"

"From the moment you got in and we started working on your hair, to the second that strange woman left your reading room, you've waxed poetic about what it might be like to swoop into his arms, fix his affair no matter who is cheating on whom, and run off into the night together."

Faith had honestly thought she and Charlotte hadn't said much to each other all day. It turns out her entire thought process may have been out loud.

"Are you sure you're not reading my mind," asked Faith. "Maybe you *should* get into the fortune telling side of things, too."

Charlotte laughed. "If there is no money in Reiki and massage, there is *definitely* no money in divination."

Faith scowled, "hey!"

CHAPTER SIX

The next morning was Saturday, and Faith had hope that business might be slightly better. Teenagers would be wondering what to do, parents would run errands together, and the big city tourists would drive over to try and blend in with small town life. She forced her subconscious to not tell her otherwise.

She slipped herself into a simple t-shirt and yoga pants and opened her apartment door.

Taped over the peephole was an eviction notice.

She tore it down and threw it on the counter, then ambled out of her apartment in the direction of the coffee shop. She'd worry about that later. She had bigger fish to fry so early on a weekend morning. Once again, the previous evening she'd forgotten to pick coffee beans up on the way home from Faye's Fortunes.

Although I had plenty of opportunity to pop out and get some during that busy day of zero customers, she lamented to herself.

If finances every improved, she promised herself she would find a cute little house and maybe order one of those fancy coffee service companies to stock the store's back office. Charlotte deserved it too, what with all the coffees she brought Faith, and all the work she put in trying to keep the business from going under.

For most people in the small town of Fallstaff, Missouri, weekends were for sleeping in. However, Saturdays were the only time to potentially make money at alternative healing, so Faith and Charlotte had agreed to wake up early and keep the store open as long as possible. They would try to catch get the weekend joggers in the morning, the curious high schoolers in the mid-afternoon, and the going-out-for-drinks crowd later in the evening. It would be a long and exhausting day, made longer without the coffee she desperately needed, but she could sleep in on Sunday when everyone in town was at church. A busy and extra-long Saturday workday would be worth it for even one more client than yesterday.

Yesterday, when her only customer was Kelsey.

Kelsey, the girlfriend of the sweet guy Faith had accidentally-but-literally fallen for.

Faith still hadn't figured out where the line was when it came to reading fortunes for someone who didn't realize how much she already knew. She felt fake, like a double agent working for her own selfish gains.

"But that's the other thing, isn't it? I don't really know much of anything," she said to the sidewalk as she crossed the street in front of her townhouse. "He's nothing but a stranger."

"Who is?" A deep and familiar voice sounded nearby. On the front porch of the cottage, Jasper's grandmother sat and smiled at her, but the voice wasn't correct for her.

I really have to practice not talking out loud to myself, Faith blushed and waved at the woman. As she approached the overgrown clematis hedge, she saw the honeyed locks of her new favorite sidewalk paver.

"Jasper," she breathed, then shook herself out of her dream-like trance.

To hide her pleasure at his presence, she tried a joke. "I don't have gemstones to rescue today, there's no need to hang out down there in the bushes."

She walked around the hedge to see him cutting away at the twigs she'd tripped over the day before. When he looked up at her, she caught his Tiger's-eye-colored irises and her heart skipped two beats. She could not help herself, and she kept staring into his beautiful eyes for a moment too long.

She felt a wave of sexuality burn deep in her belly. She completely forgot the last time she'd been in a relationship.

Jasper smiled and looked away from her. "No more flying gemstones on my watch," he laughed. "I have to leave soon for my volunteer work, but I had a bit of time to pop over and fix Gran's sidewalk."

"I'm sorry about your fall yesterday, Faith," said the woman.

How does she know my name, wondered Faith. Then she thought she saw a small blush creep across Jasper's face, too. He must have mentioned it.

The feeling in her gut turned from a few butterflies to a swarm, and she felt like she was on a wave of something between a roller coaster and a tidal wave.

Then she reminded herself that his Grandmother was there to witness the fall yesterday and probably heard her say her name. She felt her cheeks start to flush in embarrassment.

This was nothing. This meant nothing.

All of these thoughts took less than five seconds, but Faith felt awkward standing over this guy on the sidewalk and wondered what to say next. She turned toward main street and opened her mouth to say goodbye, when Jasper's grandmother stood up from her chair and asked, "would you like a tea, dear?"

"Oh!" Faith looked from main street toward the woman, "I do, but I need to go open the store. My partner is expecting me any minute."

"She will wait. Send her one of those text email thingies then," laughed the lady. She nodded toward her front door, indicating that Faith should follow her inside. "I have some things you might like to see."

Faith looked from the house toward the store, then to Jasper and to Jasper's grandmother, and decided then and there that it was very good business to befriend the neighbors and local people-watchers. Perhaps the lady knew some people to reach out to for main street business contacts.

She stepped carefully around Jasper's freshly cut twigs and the sidewalk bricks he had reset.

"It's looking good," she said to him, then berated herself for such a useless comment. Of course it was looking good, he was a professional sidewalk guy.

"You won't be tripping over this section any time soon," Jasper bragged.

"Damn! No more opportunities for nights in shining armor to catch me then, I guess."

Jasper blushed, and Faith was so overwhelmed with her quick and flirtatious comment, she failed to notice the first step up to his Grandmother's porch. Her big toe caught the lip of the old wood, and she tumbled flat onto the decking.

"Woah," said Jasper from the ground.

His Grandmother tittered, "Maybe I should get my little knight to fix the steps, too!"

"Oh geez," blushed Faith. She scampered across the front porch, completely shamefaced.

Her embarrassment was cut short when she entered the house and looked around. The small Tudor cottage was tastefully, abundantly replete with glass ornaments, gemstones, colored tiles, mirrors, and vintage knick-knacks. This house had clearly been lovingly lived in for many years and had acquired generations of family treasures.

Faith gasped in wonder. She didn't know where to move her eyes next. Being a young, broke fortune teller, it would take years to earn the resources and experience to decorate in such a magical way.

She spotted a built-in shelving unit and couldn't stop herself. She bolted over to it and ran her around a mirrored glass bowl filled with wonderous orbs of colored glass.

"It's a pagan altar," she exclaimed.

"You recognize it? My husband built that for me when we first got the house," the woman said. From what would otherwise be an antique desk, she withdrew two teacups and a selection of teas. Faith admired the way her living space had been set up just for her.

"You have such a beautiful home," Faith said after a minute, realizing she'd been quietly examining every tchotchke on every shelf and smelling the classic lived-in aroma of a mystical, well-loved home.

The woman smiled wistfully, "I have loved it for many years, but it's time to say goodbye."

"Oh no," cried Faith, surprising even herself at how devastated the statement made her feel. What would become of this magic if the magician were no longer around? "What do you mean," she asked.

The woman looked down at the kettle, which was starting to whistle. "Now that my neighbor Frannie is gone, the kids want to move me into a retirement home."

At Faith's look of fear, Jasper's grandmother continued, "Oh, it's fine, dear. It's natural. My kids and grandkids all live in Jefferson City now, so it's hard to come out here and check up on me all the time. I'm happy to move and meet some other friends like Fran. She and I always talked about having a water view one day."

She looked from the kettle out to a fairy garden by the window. "I'm only nostalgic because I'll miss this little house and all its treasures," she sighed.

"Well, let me know if you need any help packing up," Faith said. "I'll give you my number. I work at the little fortune shop -"

"-around the corner! Yes, I love that the shops on Main street are bouncing back again. I watch you walking there every morning."

Faith smiled. She had seen the woman numerous times before, and her neighbor Fran as well, but beyond a smile or wave she'd never stopped to get to know them. If she had, she may have learned of this magical cottage ages ago.

And now the woman was moving out.

"I saw you with Fran's stones yesterday," the woman said, "I'm so sorry about your fall."

"Nonsense, I'm a bit of a klutz," Faith teased herself.

"You fell at the right time; JJ was here to help you and now he's fixing my walkway today. It was fate!"

Faith blushed and looked out the front window, where Jasper was carefully cementing more sidewalk bricks into place.

"You can have this bowl of crystals, if you'd like."

"Hmm?" she'd only half heard Jasper's Grandmother.

The woman handed Faith a warm tea and went back to the kitchen to pour another.

"The glass bowl you were looking at, from the altar. You can have that and anything else you'd like," she waved her shaky hand around her living room.

Faith looked at Jasper again thinking, *I can't have everything I'd like.*

She pulled herself out of her daydream. "Oh gosh, no ma'am. I can't take your stuff!"

"You can call me Eleanor, and sure you can. If you don't take it, my kids will just sell it all at a garage sale anyway, like Fran's kids did with hers."

Faith frowned, feeling terrible. She'd bought Fran's crystals at an unbelievable bargain, but now she'd turned around and started listing them to sell at a markup.

Eleanor shook a hand at her, "Don't go feeling bad about it, dear. You got a great deal and I'm glad Fran's magical stuff can help you make your own magic now, too. In fact, I have plenty of crystals myself, you know."

Faith was taken aback, "did I think out loud again?"

"No, but you're not the only one with the gift of perception, love!" Eleanor beamed, "I promise you that Fran would be fine with you reselling her crystals. She valued the energy your new shop brought to our little corner of the world, and it's better that her treasures go to you than a stranger or the trash. She and I used to sit out on the porch with our tea and watch you walk to work every day."

"I wish I'd said more than hello," said Faith.

"You say something every day with your smile and personality." Eleanor handed Faith a second cup of tea in a vintage tasseography cup. She didn't need to say anything about it, Faith read her mind as though they were two psychics communicating wordlessly. The second cup was for her to take out to Jasper.

"What did you do before you retired," asked Faith as she headed toward the front door.

"Everything," Eleanor replied, "women do everything."

Faith opened the front door and Eleanor raised the pitch of her voice so Jasper could hear, "and the men fix the sidewalks so we can get it all done."

CHAPTER SEVEN

"I'd be offended," laughed Jasper, standing up from the sidewalk and walking to meet Faith at the foot of the porch steps, "but I enjoy pavement work. Is this good enough for now, Gran?"

He took the tea from Faith and let the mug warm his hands.

"Of course, dear, it will do for today. These fixes might even add more value to the property. Your parents will be happy about that."

Jasper frowned. "They wouldn't sell it from under you, would they? This is temporary, right?"

"Retirement homes are rarely temporary, sweet boy. But it's okay, I'm looking forward to being closer to everyone in the City and to having more people my age to talk to, now that Frannie is gone."

Faith wondered if she was out of place in this familial conversation and didn't know quite what to say. "I'm so sorry for your loss," she managed again, looking up at the other little cottage next door. She could not believe only day ago she'd purchased a beautiful collection of stones from the deceased woman's property, then promptly upended herself all over the pavement.

"It's the cycle of life, dear," Eleanor smiled from her doorway. "We're born, we find our passions, we fall in love, and we die."

Was she reading Faith's mind again? And was it Faith's imagination, or had she lingered on the love bit?

"Speaking of passions," Jasper shook cement dust off one of his hands, "They're expecting me at the zoo in an hour. I'd better clean up."

"Say hi to Naveen," laughed Eleanor.

"Who is Naveen?" As soon as the question flew out of her mouth, Faith realized she probably sounded like an envious girlfriend. Had he already broken up with Kelsey and moved on to someone else? Was Naveen the third wheel in the love affair triangle?

She prayed her rapid line of interrogation was only apparent to herself.

Luckily, Jasper didn't seem to notice. With pride, he exclaimed, "Naveen is one of my seals at the zoo. She's pregnant!"

Faith caught a twinkle in Eleanor's eye. Jasper might not have caught her envious thought stream, but his Grandmother had.

Faith felt her cheeks darken and she blurted, "Wow, neat, good luck to her. Pregnant? Gosh. What a thing. Okay, I have to get to work too now."

Slow down woman, she castigated herself.

Slower, she asked Eleanor, "Can I come in and wash out my cup?"

"I have to wash some sidewalk off of myself, so I'll take that in." Jasper reached his hand out for her cup just as she started holding it up to show Eleanor. His knuckles brushed Faith's and another small bolt of electricity shocked both of them again. She wondered if she'd just imagined it this time.

"Must be electrified pavement," Jasper laughed. He'd felt it too.

"Thank you for the tea," Faith hurriedly gushed to Eleanor, and she turned to dart away before her now rapid heartbeat and flushed cheeks gave her dirty thoughts away any further. She was melting into a complete mess and just needed to get to work.

"Please drop by any time, dear," called Eleanor from the porch. "You can look through my things to see what else might work in your store. It will be such fun!"

Faith's eyes shot from Eleanor to Jasper, and she saw him scowl as he entered the house. Did he know Eleanor had offered Faith her occult items? How did he feel about it? Did he know about his family's plan to sell her belongings, move her out, and get control of her house?

She did not have time to try and read Jasper's mind, so instead she spun around and got out of there as quickly as possible. She had a store to run and a business partner depending on her.

As she raced down the street, she reminded herself that as an overworked and broke businesswoman, she did not have the freedom to follow up on silly crushes, get involved in family legacy issues, wonder about client affairs, discuss pregnant seals, or trip over any more damn sidewalks.

She made sure to watch her steps carefully this time as she bolted toward Main street and away from whatever *that* was this morning.

When she rounded the shop's corner she all but ran into Charlotte, who was yelling a string of obscenities at a truck driver.

Faith stumbled, and when she got her bearings, she saw the devastation behind them - the truck had backed up over the curb and smashed most of their beautiful glass-lined sidewalk.

"Fuuuu--n," Faith breathed out. She kicked a patch of broken glass and concrete and marched into the shop.

CHAPTER EIGHT

"Well, that guy is certain his insurance will cover it, but it's a real mess out there," Charlotte called as she approached the back office.

Faith sat in front of the mirror, trying to insert feathers into her own hair and failing miserably.

Charlotte was much better at turning Faith into Faye, and it was obvious she recognized that skill when she rounded the corner into the room. She let out a long rumble and shook her head.

"Nuh-uh," she waved Faith's hands away and took over the head feathers.

Faith cheered, "What am I ever going to do without you?"

"Why would you say that? Am I dying? You'd better not be ending our partnership. I just spent the last half hour screaming at a truck driver for ruining our entryway, so I'm doing my part."

"No, silly goose, I would never break up with you! But if we keep losing money like this, there isn't going to be a shop for us to be partners in."

"Then you'll be the one out on your butt," Charlotte deftly replaced some of the feathers Faith had not inserted properly, "I'm the one making the most money here."

Faith frowned. Although she was kidding, Charlotte was right. She was currently the one floating them, as her massage business got more customers and higher pay.

Faith dusted some powder over her face. "Maybe instead of a fortune shop offering massages, we should change it to a massage parlor offering tarot readings."

"Nah," Charlotte scoffed, finishing the feathers and moving on to applying Faye's heavy green and blue eyeshadow. "Creeps would mistake a massage place for a sex shop or something. I like my current clientele; I just need more of them. They'll come."

"I admire your positivity," Faith said, but she didn't feel any herself.

Within a few minutes, she was fully transformed into Faye. She threw a blue and green shimmering robe over her t-shirt and tights, and she was unrecognizable as her former self again. Faye Sybella twirled with a smoothness and confidence that Faith Sybertz would certainly trip over if confidence were cracks in the pavement.

"Speaking of pavement," Faye sang, as if their conversation had never strayed from the broken sidewalk, "let me see what kind of damage was done out there."

"Dressed like that?" Charlotte eyed her conspicuously.

For a darkened fortune telling sanctuary, Faye was perfectly, majestically adorned. But for a bright Saturday morning on the streets of Fallstaff, Missouri, she was extremely out of place.

She faked a commanding bellow, "I am the all-knowing oracle of a divination shop, and I declare that walking outside to survey my lands shall invoke the great spirit to send customers my way." Her robes danced as though an invisible breeze had struck only her.

Truthfully, a small twist of her wrists shifted the fine robe material just enough to make it look like a mysterious wind had caught it.

Charlotte had seen this trick done many times before. She shook her head and retorted, "alright then, magic lady. You go outside and use your psychic powers to create some customers. I'm going to prep my massage table. Maybe if I sprinkle it with extra love I can invoke the spirits to send me some customers, too."

"Watch it with the love sprinkling," Faye teased, "we run a clean business here."

Faye danced herself over to the shop door and whisked it open with another fake flourish designed to entertain Charlotte.

She almost danced right into Kelsey, who stood prepped with her hand ready to grab the door handle.

Kelsey's jaw drop could have hit the already busted pavement. She gushed, "how'd you know I was here?"

Although startled, Faye composed herself quickly and lowered her voice, "I know everything." She stepped backward into the shop and waved her robed arm, "Please, do come in again my child."

Out of the corner of her eye, Faye caught Charlotte shaking her head as she ducked into her massage studio. Faye didn't need to be a psychic to know there was an eyeroll, too.

CHAPTER NINE

Kelsey was clearly panicked, and she hurried into the reading room to sit in the correct chair this time. With silent relief, Faye took her power seat behind her crystal ball.

"So," Faye inquired of the distraught woman, "what is your concern today?"

"Well, now I'm worried about that three of swords card from the other day," Kelsey said. "Do you see anything about <u>Jacob</u> cheating on <u>me</u>?"

Faye almost fell out of character as she shook her head in confusion. Was Kelsey cheating on Jasper? Or was he cheating on her? Was Faith's flirtation with Jasper getting too serious? Who was Jacob?

No, wait, Jacob is Jasper! Faith had briefly forgotten that Kelsey used his second name when she spoke to him, for reasons Faith still did not fully understand.

She shook her head at her own silliness. Kelsey didn't know she'd talked to Jasper again that morning. She still hadn't recognized her at all from the day before.

With wide eyes, Kelsey asked "What? What do you see?"

Faith realized that all the while she'd been chastising herself, Kelsey thought she was visualizing something in the crystal ball again, not trying to figure out who Jacob was and what was going on.

"I see-" she slowed her voice and got back into character, moving her head in slow circles and closing her eyes, "I see a woman."

"What?! What type of woman? Who is she?" Kelsey's face darkened with rage in the already dim reading room.

"Her name is," Faye flitted her hands around her crystal orb and opened one eye to see if Kelsey was paying attention, "Naveen."

"Naveen?" Kelsey furrowed her brow as if trying to solve an algebra problem.

Faye wondered how long it would take her to do the calculation required to remember Jasper's pregnant seal.

But Kelsey never got there, which meant she either didn't know about the seal, or she'd forgotten. That told Faye everything she needed to know about how invested Kelsey was in her relationship with Jasper.

Not needing further insight, Kelsey threw twenty bucks on the table and stood to march out of the room. "That bastard!"

Wanting to ease her mind, Faye chased her through the reception room and out the shop door, where they bumped directly into Jasper.

The shock spun them all into momentary silence. Faye noticed Charlotte's eyeball peering out from the doorway to her massage room. She smiled sympathetically, and then disappeared.

"Hey, what's up with this sidewalk?" Jasper smiled nervously. "I saw you come in here on my way to the z--"

"You bastard," Kelsey repeated. "Who the hell is Naveen?"

"Naveen?" Jasper looked from Kelsey to Faye. "Naveen," he repeated.

Faye felt her cheeks flush. Her jig was up, and she saw the recognition in Jasper's face. Everything he'd said to her that morning was now being repeated back to Kelsey, and not only was it proof that Kelsey didn't listen to anything he told her about his volunteer work with the zoo, it was also proof that Faith was using that information for her job as Kelsey's psychic.

In that brief interaction, Faith became the oracle she'd struggled to be for the previous few weeks, and she saw the entire future laid out as clear as the daylight: The couple in front of her would break up. The bricklayer-slash-zoo volunteer would realize his girlfriend didn't care about or pay any attention to his passions. The girlfriend would accuse him of cheating and play that up to gain sympathies from some other sucker. And the fortune teller would retreat to her bankrupt shop to try and pick up whatever pieces were left to salvage.

There was a lot to salvage: broken glass stones from the sidewalk, unpaid bills from a bank that would soon foreclose on her, and a very humiliated and broken heart.

In a daze, Faye left the fighting couple and retreated into the shop.

"It was bound to happen," Charlotte said. She closed the reception window curtains from where she'd obviously been spying, "you probably aren't the first Psychic to ruin a relationship, and you won't be the last."

CHAPTER TEN

Almost a week went by with no sign of Kelsey, Jasper, nor even Eleanor waving from her front porch. Faith wondered if the family had moved her out already, and what was to come of her unique eclectic belongings.

Faith had been so embarrassed about the incident with Kelsey and Jasper, she had not taken Eleanor up on her offer to browse the collection of metaphysical items, even though she desperately wanted to.

Her biggest problem wasn't love, or relationships, or magical stuff, it was Faye's Fortunes itself. The store wasn't making any money and Charlotte and Faith had spent the week fielding phone calls from creditors. Charlotte could count on one hand the regulars she'd seen that week, and neither she nor Faith had seen many walk-ins. A few teenagers had popped in on Monday afternoon, but because they were visiting a psychic against their parents' wishes, Faith had taken whatever measly hot dog money they could Venmo her, rather than her full fees. One woman had rushed in frantic about having lost her job, but because the poor thing was unemployed Faith had accepted only five bucks and given her a free aventurine crystal to help manifest job success.

"We can't keep giving discounts and freebies," Faith said on Friday morning, as Charlotte fumbled through drawers looking for better feathers. The feathers in Faith's hair were starting to get ratty, but without money to spend on new ones, they had to be reused every time.

"I'd be happy to charge full price if we could get some wallets in the front door," Charlotte retorted, slamming a drawer.

She relaxed her shoulders and tried another drawer. "I'm sorry, I'm just as frustrated as you are."

Faith wasn't bothered by Charlotte's snappy attitude; she'd come to expect it in the absence of customers, and she was often just as short-tempered herself.

"No, I'm sorry, Charlie. You're the one with actual regular clients. I should be busting ass to get us more business while you're working."

"You're doing enough. We both are," Charlotte admitted.

It was true. They had posted all over social media, they'd forked over as much pocket change as they could for an advertisement in the local paper, and Charlotte had even gotten a short speaking gig on a holistic wellness podcast. But none of it had helped.

Charlotte tried to fix a broken feather with a toothpick and scotch tape.

"We could move the shop to Jefferson City," Faith said, dusting her eyes with blue shadow. "I think this small town just can't handle a divination and alternative health store."

"Oh yeah, with what money would we use to relocate a store?" Charlotte pushed the repaired feather into the back of Faith's head with a bit more oomph than usual.

Faith winced, and both women sighed. The feather flopped.

But within a few minutes, girl-next-door Faith had been transformed into magical and mysterious Faye, only with slightly uglier feathers than usual.

Just as Charlotte was putting a final twisted feather into her hair, the door of the shop chimed.

The women smiled at each other in the mirror and in silent agreement they shook away their negativity. "Let's get this," said Charlotte.

Faye stood up with grace and composure and floated toward the office door. Charlotte began stretching her shoulders in case it was a drop-in massage client.

"Ah, our esteemed client awaits" Faye fluttered as she exited the back office, speaking toward Charlotte but aiming her voice loudly toward the door, hoping the customer would hear it and feel as though they were expected, psychically.

Jasper stood by the shop door and waved at her, a shy smile across his face.

CHAPTER ELEVEN

"Jasper. I didn't expect to ever see-"

Faith stumbled over a string of Faye's robe and found her face hurtling toward the floor.

Jasper reacted immediately and caught her mid-tumble.

"Wow, you're fast," she said, clutching at his biceps.

She instantly felt ridiculous about saying such a silly thing.

"You learn to be quick working with the seals," Jasper said, "they're always getting underfoot while I'm cleaning their cages."

"Right, the seals." Faith remembered how she'd used that information in the reading for Kelsey, and what a scam artist she must look like to everyone involved.

She had so many questions she wanted to ask - whether his relationship had survived, whether Kelsey was mad at her, whether they'd split in a terrible rage like the three of swords had foretold, which one of them was having the affair she'd predicted (or was she completely wrong about that), but all she could get out was "How are they? The seals, I mean."

Jasper made sure she was steady, then let go.

"They're good. Last weekend I was heading in to check on Naveen, when-"

He fell silent.

Faith nodded and felt her cheeks flush. She looked down at the floor in humiliation and was glad the lights in the reception room were dim. Her face would easily betray her in the light.

Right. Last week when I carelessly destroyed everything for all of us.

"Well," she said, re-composing herself from Faith-the asshole into Faye-the fortune teller extraordinaire.

Faye asked, "How can I help you today?"

Jasper's lips seemed poised to say something important, but he shook his head and looked down.

Faye kept her chin up and smiled, but inside Faith was collapsing into pieces.

Jasper appeared to pivot from whatever topic was at the forefront of his mind. "I was wondering if I could get some water from you," he said with zero emotion.

"You're thirsty?" Faye asked, moving behind a glass cabinet full of baubles and candles. She uncovered a small mini fridge hidden under the counter.

"No," Jasper stopped her. He picked up a bucket he'd placed by the front door. "I mean a bucket of water, for the cement."

"What cement?"

"Outside."

Faye stared at him for too many seconds, then she nodded in understanding.

"Insurance must have approved the repair," she stated in monotone.

"And I'm the only sidewalk game in town," Jasper repeated her emotionless speech.

Faye nodded and waved toward the corner of the room, "The bathroom is just there, behind the curtain." She indicated an excess of material hung against the wall.

In a soft voice she said, "the handle is a bit hard to find, because-"

"-because hiding a bathroom gives the appearance of mystery," Jasper glowered, "I get it."

He fumbled for the handle and disappeared into the bathroom, slamming the door.

Faye's shoulders fell. He was angry at her, and it would be too much to try and explain to him that yes, this was a business which needed to uphold an air of mystery for its clients, but that she's also an empathic human who can clearly see that he's pissed at her and that she made a stupid mistake and she's sorry.

It had been a crime of opportunity.

Guaranteed had she not known Jasper or Kelsey, the Tarot cards or Runes or crystal ball or tea leaves or any perceptive person in the entire would have predicted the same future about the two of them eventually breaking up, but having an extra bit of insider assistance when doing a reading of that caliber never hurt Faye.

But it had hurt Faith.

She fled to the back office, where Charlotte held the door open for her.

"Did you hear all that?" Faye asked.

"I didn't need to hear it, hon. I felt it," Charlotte said.

CHAPTER TWELVE

The rest of the morning brought another whopping zero customers into the shop. Faith wished she could blame the construction crew fixing the sidewalk outside, but she knew it wouldn't matter if they were there or not. Business just wasn't good, and it might never become good.

She adjusted some of the crystals on the shelves, wondering if proper Feng Shui placement might bring in more customers. She moved a large black obsidian sphere to a spot by the front window, where Charlotte was peering out through the curtains.

"Yum-meee" Charlotte licked her lips. "I do love me some construction workers."

Faith still felt terrible about how everything had gone down with Jasper, but she couldn't help chuckling at her friend.

Charlotte shifted her body out of the way to make room for Faith to also watch the crew working on the ground outside.

Faith shook her head *no*.

"Come on, bestie," Charlotte playfully smacked her shoulder, "Just because you're sad doesn't mean you can't get some good eye candy in. Besides, your little man crush isn't out there anymore."

"What?" Faith moved to the window to see for herself.

Outside were two men polishing up a finished sidewalk, and Jasper was nowhere in sight.

"I told you they were handsome," Charlotte nodded at the specimens and licked her top lip.

Faith was no longer paying attention to them. Where had Jasper gone? He was the only good sidewalk guy in Fallstaff, Missouri. He'd said so himself. It didn't seem like him to skip out on a job like this, especially when he'd raved about how unique the glass stones were.

Charlotte huffed. "Hey, if you're not interested in our construction crew, I'll take 'em both."

She opened the door and the shop bells chimed as though mirroring her horny glee. "Hey boys," she said in a smooth, silky voice, "thanks for your hard work. Can I interest either of you in a shoulder massage?"

Both the men blushed.

"No funny business, I promise your... wives?" Charlotte teased, trying and failing to keep it clean, while covertly searching for their marital statuses. "We just wanted to say thank you for fixing our entryway."

Faith couldn't hear what the men said to Charlotte, but it seemed affirmative.

"Good. I promise it's all on the up and up," Charlotte smiled and stood back in the doorway. To the taller construction worker she teased, "unless you're interested."

"Just some water would be fine, ma'am" said the shorter one, eyeing Faith's Faye outfit as they entered.

Faith had forgotten who she was for a moment, but she straightened up quickly. "Of course," she sang in Faye's deep timbre, and she drifted her body behind the counter to grab two water bottles.

She handed the first bottle to the taller construction worker. A tiny shock tickled the two of them, and Faye had a mini vision - her first real psychic moment in quite a while.

"Your heart was recently broken by a powerful man," she said, equally confused as he was that her gifts had chosen that moment to start coming back.

The man jumped back and hugged the water close to his body. "Uh, yeah. Thanks for reminding me, I guess."

The shorter, stockier man laughed and hit him across the chest "a man, huh Chris? Wait'll the team hears this!" He continued to laugh and shake his head.

Charlotte stepped in between them and smiled sweetly at the taller construction worker, Chris. "You'll have to excuse my psychic friend," she glowered at Faye as she added, "She shouldn't be working for free anyway."

Faye dropped the subject quickly and snapped herself out of her trance. Two burly construction workers probably wouldn't have the patience nor understanding for the otherworldly arts, where oracle minds like Faye's spent half their lives.

Even Charlotte barely understood it, and she was a partner in Faye's shop.

"I'm sorry," Faye blurted out, "I need to stop speaking when I'm not asked. Please do come again."

She held the door for the workers as they left, the short one still shaking his head and laughing. The tall one, Chris, scowled down at her as he passed.

When the door was closed, Charlotte made sure the men were gone and interrogated Faye. "What the hell was that about, woman?"

"I think my second sight is coming back," Faye grinned, relieved.

Charlotte did not seem convinced. She smirked, "That's great. Do you foresee any paying customers in our future?"

Faye sighed, "Okay, maybe it's not all the way back."

"Then stop scaring off the only customers we've got!"

CHAPTER THIRTEEN

Saturday morning, Faith woke up feeling different. It was as if her confidence had returned overnight, and the neurons for her fortune telling powers had started to heal themselves.

The eviction notice still loomed on her kitchen counter, but this time she didn't look at it with regret and sadness, just a strange inner feeling that everything was going to be work out the way it should. She'd always thought her ugly townhouse apartment had bad mojo, now this was a sign that she'd be able to get out sooner rather than later.

She bounded down the front steps and skipped across the street hurriedly, as though her entire side of the street was cursed, and Eleanor's side was blessed.

A subtle note from her subconscious tried to remind her that this side of the street had brought her nothing but accidents, mistakes, and romantic doom, but she brushed it off when a small voice sang "hello!"

Eleanor sat on her front porch, almost invisible by her overgrowing hedge. She waved Faith over to sit with her. "Do you have time for a cup of tea before work, dear?"

"Always," Faith replied with a smile, although the actual truth was that she only had time because her shop never had any customers.

Eleanor seemed to silently understand this and fluffed up a pillow for her guest to sit for a spell.

As Faith ascended the steps, she saw a teapot and two cups already laid out in front of the woman. Her eyes widened, "did you-"

"-did I know you'd come for tea? Of course, dear. You're not the only empath in town."

Faye took her seat in an aging wicker rocker and poured herself a cup. The fresh scents of bergamot and citrus wafted into her senses and seemed to feed her brainwaves. She gave herself a reminder to try tea instead of coffee before Tarot readings, to see if she could keep her innate senses running at optimal efficiency.

"You can have what's in my tea cabinet," Eleanor said.

Faith was stupefied. *Could this woman be an actual psychic with the power to see inside others' heads?*

She asked, "are you reading my mind?"

Eleanor laughed, the kind of sweet elderly giggle that infected everyone around her. "Of course not, silly girl. But the look on your face as you inhaled the tea was a sure sign that a pleasant morning on a porch like this is something you need more of in your life."

Faith smiled but looked away from the woman to try and hide a growing sense of regret.

Eleanor tilted her head forward to get Faith's attention back, and to indicate that talking to her was safe and welcome.

"I'm probably going to lose the shop. I've already lost my apartment," Faith tilted her chin toward her townhouse across the street. From this vantage point, the building looked even more sinister and out of place.

"I never liked that house anyway," said Eleanor. "I hope they tear it down and rebuild something that fits in with the neighborhood."

Faith nodded. "You and Miss Francis got the best houses on the block, that's for sure. I wonder what will come of them, now that-"

Faith tried to drop her thought stream. She did not want to further upset this woman who had just lost her best friend, and who was probably on the verge of being moved out very soon, herself.

She looked over toward Francis' property and saw the for-sale sign had been moved. It may already have been sold to a developer.

"It's fine. A nice couple bought it," Eleanor said from her seat, watching Faith.

"Stop reading my mind," Faith commanded, half joking but also quite suspicious.

"The thing about being an empath," Eleanor said, "is that it's not about reading minds, it's about picking up on context clues and running with them. But you know that already, don't you?"

Faith nodded, and felt an embarrassing tear start to sting her eye. Why did this make her sad, and why did she feel so comfortable being vulnerable with Eleanor?

"You had these gifts, so you opened a store to share them with the world," Eleanor continued.

"But nobody came," Faith lamented.

"Life isn't a 1980s Kevin Costner movie," Eleanor joked. "You can't build it and they will just come. Businesses grow and fail all the time, sometimes no matter what you do. You did all the right things, but maybe Fallstaff wasn't ready for it, yet. They will be, but you must remember to charge what your skills are worth. People will want to pay you when they see what you can do. They want to get their money's worth, so don't sell yourself short."

Faith sat back, folding into herself and wondering if she should close the store and give her dream up. "Do you really think business will improve?"

"I absolutely know it will!"

Eleanor took notice of Faith's wide eyes again, "and before you ask, it's not because I'm psychic. It's because I know something you don't. Knowing things is part of what being an empath is, isn't it?"

Faith realized Eleanor was talking about Jasper's relationship, and how she'd used her insider knowledge to astonish Kelsey. She felt her cheeks darken.

"It's fine, dear. It's all part of the business. It doesn't make you a fraud to utilize what you know in your business. It makes you a good, understanding listener. Now, come with me-" Eleanor stood and indicated that Faith should come into the house with her.

"I should really get to work," Faith nodded over her shoulder toward Main street.

"Not until you take some of this stuff to sell in your shop, you won't," Eleanor said. "I purposefully held a bunch of my old stuff back from the movers so that you could have it. A lot of it has some really good value, in case any fancy big city antiques shoppers come to our little town. I also have some cute little trinkets for the town's children. There is plenty here to keep your business alive."

"You're so generous, Eleanor, I couldn't possibly-"

"Oh, now. Don't go thinking I'm the most altruistic grandma on the block. I have my own desires at heart. Fallstaff is my hometown, and I love it so. After my kids move me to Jefferson City, I want to make sure this little town thrives in whatever way possible, so that maybe the following generation moves back some day."

She winked at Faith as she opened her front door. She meant Jasper, her grandson.

Eleanor continued, "So that might mean sharing my stuff with the little shops on Main street, or maybe tearing down ugly apartment complexes built in the fifties," she waved at Faith's soon-to-be-former building.

Faith glared at her as the two stepped into the house. "Did you get me evicted?"

Eleanor beamed. "All I said was that nobody is truly altruistic. Everyone ultimately has their own self-interest at heart. Now, come along."

Faith didn't know whether to storm away or thank the woman for shaking up her life, so instead she shrugged and followed Eleanor into her living room.

She saw that most of the furniture and the myriad of knickknacks had been cleared out already. But in the corner of the living room was a huge stack of boxes all labeled "Faith's fortune."

Her eyes widened. She was too shocked by the number of boxes to point out that her shop was actually called *Faye's Fortunes*. She had an inkling that Eleanor knew that well enough.

"Do you want to look at it all, to make sure it suits the shop?"

Faith took a few seconds to realize the old woman was talking to her. She shook her head. "I already know it does," she said with certainty, "all of it is perfect. I feel it in my bones."

Eleanor's eyes twinkled.

Faith realized it was quite a haul. Despite the shop being only a block away, she didn't have the time nor strength to carry it all. "I guess I'll bring one box with me now, and maybe figure out a rental truck or lorry or something."

"No need," Eleanor said, "the boys can bring it over later."

Before Faith could ask what she meant by boys, Eleanor waved her hands as if to scoot her off, "now, off you go, the shop is already open for business!"

What business, Faith wondered, but she grabbed a box and let Eleanor shoo her out of the house.

"And watch your step," Eleanor giggled as Faith stepped out onto the sidewalk.

"Thankfully, your grandson did a fairly good sidewalk patch job," Faith skipped down the stairs.

As she walked on the freshly dried concrete, she wondered how Jasper was doing.

She didn't need to wonder for long, because when she rounded the corner on Main street, she saw him and several other people standing outside her store. She recognized the tall construction worker, Chris, and saw Charlie flirting with him in the doorway.

"Oh no," Faith hesitated, then hurried toward the door and started to ask, "Did something happen to the sidewalk agai-"

"Woman, get your butt over here!" Charlie called when she spotted her. "We've got a line!"

CHAPTER FOURTEEN

The crowd parted as Faith approached the shop. Jasper gave her a small nod as she approached, but he stayed back. He was either partway through a discussion with a coworker, or he'd started a new one to avoid her. Faith tried to convince herself it meant nothing.

To Charlotte, Faith whispered, "What is everyone doing here?"

Chris stepped in, "I need to talk to you about what you saw the other day."

"What did I see? Oh, your heartbreak?" Faith put a hand on his arm, "I'm so very sorry I outed you. I was way out of line-"

"But how did you know? Nobody knew!"

His partner, the shorter construction worker, playfully swatted him on the arm. "We've been working with this guy for six months and he's never told us he's gay. The entire team is offended! We want to know more secrets!"

A woman called out from behind them, "Nobody wants to know *your* secrets, Bill. I'm just here for a goddamn massage."

Charlie smiled and held up a clipboard "My ears are burning! Let me start writing down names."

"I'll go in and get dressed, I guess" Faith said, shifting the box under one arm so she could open the door.

Jasper spoke for the first time, "You don't need the feathers, if that's what you're suggesting."

Faith turned to look at him. The crowd watched her, nodding in agreement.

Chris said, "he's right. We just want to get some hope for our lives today, we don't need to wait for all that woo-woo shit."

Charlie smiled, "I could use a day off from the hair, to be honest. Besides, a bit of income today will buy better feathers for tomorrow."

Chris reached for the cardboard box in Faith's hands.

She'd almost forgotten it was there, but Chris's assistance reminded her of the rest of Eleanor's gift.

Faith said, "I'm definitely not one to turn down income on what could be our best day ever, but-"

"But?" Charlie glared at her.

Faith continued, "-I'd be happy to do some free-"

"-*discounted*," Charlie grumbled.

"-discounted fortune telling for anyone who can help me carry more of these boxes from up the street."

Charlie took the box from Chris, to free him up to go get more. To Faith, she said "Hon, what does this mean? Did the eviction go through early? Are you moving into the store?"

"What? No. Gosh no," Faith laughed. "My friend Eleanor-"

"Grandma?" Jasper pushed his way forward through the crowd, "she's alright, right?"

"Yes, she's fine. I had tea with her this morning. She's set aside a bunch of stuff for our store, and there are tons of boxes, and they're heavy!"

"We're on it," the short guy, Bill, waved some of the others toward Eleanor's house.

"I'm glad you're finally working on something, Bill" another construction worker joked, and the two started up the street.

"Wait up," Jasper called to them.

Chris started to follow them.

"No no, you're with me," Faith reached out to hold Chris back. "I'm suddenly having the insight that your little broken heart needs a bit of healing right now."

Charlie carried the box in and nodded for the female construction worker to follow her, "You're with me, babe. These fingers won't massage themselves!"

CHAPTER FIFTEEN

Faith felt a bit awkward.

Sitting in Faye's velvet chair, tiny streams of morning light coming through the otherwise darkened curtains, she felt out of place in her t-shirt and jeans, with her hair in a top knot rather than flowing with feathers around her face. She could feel her face devoid of makeup. It was strange to be so normal and do a mystical psychic reading.

But maybe a little bit of normal Faith is exactly what I need to get my empathic abilities going again, her intuition all but shouted out to her.

She watched Chris fold his long legs under her small table, and the tablecloth moved a bit, tipping her bowl of Futhark Runes precariously close to the edge of the table.

"Sorry," Chris said, as Faith reached out to grab them.

"Not at all, I think the Runes are saying they want to be read today," she smiled.

She made a mental note to find a taller reading table, for future tall and brawny customers. She felt confident they would be coming now and that

Eleanor was right. She just had to trust both herself and her little occult shop in the middle of nowhere.

Faith collected the Runes and put them in a small leather satchel. She handed it to Chris to shake. "It puts your energy into them," she said to him.

He grunted, "I don't know what that means."

He was clearly not a believer but something she'd said the other day must have struck a chord. She had to keep going with it.

"While you mix those, let me tell you what I can see about you."

His shaking slowed and he raised an eyebrow at her.

"You had your heart broken by a man," she continued, the light from between the curtains catching her attention, "but it wasn't a lover like your coworkers tease you about."

He didn't give any notification that she was correct, and a week ago she would have felt vulnerable and second-guessed herself, but today she felt confident that what she was saying was spot on.

With resolve, she continued. "It was someone even closer than that. A loved *one*, not a lov*er*. A family member."

His eyes stopped watching her and dropped to the ground. He whispered, "it's my-"

"It's your-" she said at the same time,

"Father," they said simultaneously.

"Here," Faith held out a hand to take the stones back, "The Runes are the perfect tool to look at this problem more closely. They are the ancient stones of the Norse men and are the all-knowing divination tool of one of the most powerful fathers himself, Odin."

"I'm a Christian," Chris scowled, but there was a light and curious tone behind his comment.

"It's okay," Faith laughed, "I won't try and send you to Asgard to be initiated to the Norse gods or anything like that."

"Well, Asgard was blown up in that Avengers movie so that would be impossible anyway."

Now it was Faith's turn to scowl.

Chris winked at her, and she couldn't help but laugh.

"Okay, carry on," he said, "let's see what father Odin has to say about my crummy Dad."

He went to place the bag in her hand, but before she could grab it three stones came tumbling out as though they'd been commanded to line up in a perfect order. It was a reading of The Three Norns, or the Past, Present, and Future.

"Nyd," Faith read the stone representing the past. "You and your Dad had a falling out because one of you needed to break free and be anywhere else."

"That was him. Literally went out for a jug of milk and never came back. Not until-"

Chris stopped talking, perhaps still critical and not wanting to give anything away. Something caught Faith's eye in the window, but she immediately moved on to the next stone.

"Lagus reversed. He's back now and he needs something."

"And it ain't milk," Chris joked, but there was sadness behind it.

"He's broken your heart because you thought maybe he'd had a change of one, but he's just the same guy who walked out years ago," Faye stated. She wasn't a therapist, and this was something he'd have to work out with one if he couldn't face his emotions himself, but her job was not to deal with the past but to give him hope for the future.

Chris shook his head, as if reading her mind. "I probably need a shrink, not a-"

"-a woo-woo psychic?"

She could see a soft blush fall across his already dark cheeks.

"Sorry," he said.

She laughed.

"It's fine. I know what I am," Faith said with confidence. In that moment, she did know who she was. She was Faith Sybertz, and she had a gift of empathy to share with the world.

"I'm not here to make you cry over your past," Faith told him. Then she winked, "that's the shrink's job."

His furrowed brow broke, and it was his turn to chuckle.

She continued, "I'm here to guide you toward your future, whether it be good or bad. Are you ready?"

"Ready," he sat up a little straighter, and his body language indicated to Faith that maybe he was slowly coming around to believing in some of the *woo-woo psychic* stuff. The future was where it got real.

"The final Rune is Thurisaz. Ooh," Faith couldn't help but be relieved that it wasn't devastating news.

"Chris crossed his arms in what seemed like frustration, but Faith could tell he was just playing with her.

"Since you enjoy those movies, you'll love this," she continued. "Thurisaz is Thor's Rune. It's the rune of Thor and it literally translates to Thorn."

"Thor. Thor thor thor, okay," Chris said critically, "and that means what, exactly? Thor's going to come and stab my dad with a thorn?"

He moved to pick up the rock but paused, waiting for an okay before touching it. Faith nodded and smiled. The fact that he'd waited told her that although he was being a skeptic, he was still divinely interested and perhaps even starting to become aware of the powerful effect of the Rune stones.

He picked it up and looked at it.

"No," Faith assured him. "Thor probably won't come down and strike your father with lighting," she laughed. Chris scowled, so she continued, "But you must become him."

"Become Thor? I don't think it works like that. I would need that hammer."

"I mean adopt his persona. Protect your house. Protect your mother, and your mischievous brother, and-"

78

"I actually do have a mischievous brother," Chris said, surprised. "He was only a baby when Dad left, so he barely remembers it."

"It affected him, though. And you took note of that," Faith stated. "And that's why you need to be the thorn in your Dad's side."

"Be the thorn," Chris repeated. "I think I can do that. Thanks for reading my mind, shrink!"

"I'm not a shrink!" Faith exclaimed, starting to stand. "And I can't read your mind."

"But I can read yours," Chris said.

Faith stopped moving, wondering what he meant. She watched him with a raised eyebrow.

"You have a crush on my boss, Jasper."

"Get out of here," she teased and waved toward the door. But then she dropped her shoulders with concern, "am I that obvious?"

"Not to him, don't worry. I just picked up on it earlier this morning when you kept watching him out of the corner of your eye. And just now, you keep looking through the crack in the curtains as though you're looking for someone."

Now it was Faith's turn to question everything. "You wouldn't believe me if I said I was just looking out for the boxes from his Grandmother's place, would you?"

"No, I would not," Chris teased.

"You're pretty intuitive, Chris. You'd make a good psychic yourself," Faith winked, "if you're ever looking to change jobs."

"I'll keep that in mind," he stood from his seat and Faith followed him toward the door. He asked, "How much do I owe you for this?"

Faith almost said, 'it's on the house,' then something in the back of her mind told her to request the full price. She remembered Eleanor's words - people want to feel like they are purchasing something of value and getting their money's worth.

"Twenty-five bucks," Faith stated with confidence. Inside, she was nervous.

Chris pulled cash from his pocket and counted it out without even flinching. "That's pretty cheap for therapy," he laughed, handing it to her.

"Happy to help any time. I mean it," she opened the door for him and saw his friends and coworkers milling about in the reception room. "but you need to get out, now. Apparently, I have a line!"

Chris faked a complaint, "a shrink wouldn't scoot me out this quickly!"

"Good thing I'm not a shrink. Now get out of here, Thor," she mocked him back. "Okay, who's next?"

At that moment, Jasper walked out from behind some of Eleanor's boxes and said, "if no one minds, I'd love a reading right now."

CHAPTER SIXTEEN

Faith's heart just about leapt out of her chest, but not in a sweet way. It felt more like the crushing weight of a billion tarot cards and a ton of shame had barreled down on her from the sky.

She wondered how she could do a reading for someone whose life she'd so completely messed up a week ago. She already knew too much about him, and her feelings for him, and knew that a reading for him would be swayed by her own opinions.

"I don't know if it's a good idea," she said bravely.

"No? I think it's a great idea," he replied, staring her down.

The other guests in the reception room seemed to fade away. She could tell he was angry about everything that had gone down, yet he was also curious about how it all worked.

On his way out of the shop, Chris patted Jasper on the back. "Careful what you wish for, man, she's good. She can see right through you."

"I know she can," Jasper said over his shoulder without taking his eyes off Faith. "That's exactly why I'm here."

If Faith felt naked without Faye's robes before, she felt even more vulnerable now. Softly, she opened the door to her reading room and indicated for Jasper to enter and sit down. Then she fumbled with her hands, wondering whether to hang them beside her body, or hold them in front of herself like an 18th century schoolgirl, or play with loose hair hanging by her face, or what.

She settled on rushing to sit down, then she brushed invisible dust off the table in front of her.

She half laughed, half coughed, "Okay, then. Let's do this."

"Let's do it." Jasper kept watching her.

She looked anywhere but his amber eyes and started to babble, "what kind of reading would you like? I have Runes, and a crystal ball, and tea leaves - although the tea takes a minute to brew, and there's-"

"Tarot," he said, "Give me the cards."

"Oh?" She tried to be nonchalant, "are you familiar with Tarot?"

She felt Jasper stare at her, and her flesh began to heat up.

"What I know about Tarot is that my ex-girlfriend raved about it, right before we-," he paused and bore daggers into her soul. "Well, you know. Anyway, beyond that I'm very much unschooled on what it is."

"Uh, well let's see," Faith stammered as she started shuffling a deck, "Tarot was invented in the 15th century in Italy, and-"

"No, I don't care about the historical stuff right now," Jasper groused, "what I want to know is why the cards would suggest an affair was happening in my relationship."

Faith felt affronted and slightly confused. "That's not what happened at all," she stated flatly.

"Then what *did* happen?"

She looked through the deck and pulled out the three of swords, then tossed it at him and set the deck back down again. "What happened was that Kelsey drew the three of swords - of her own volition, by the way, she was very grabby, and-"

Now it was Jasper's turn to be grabby. He picked up the card and glared into it. "Looks like three swords stabbed through a heart. Pretty gruesome, isn't it? Why didn't you suggest she stab me three times and get it over with?"

"A stabbing isn't quite what that card implies!"

"Well, which card *does* imply a stabbing? Show me that one!" Jasper picked up the tarot deck and started rifling through the cards.

Faith had to think about it, "I don't know, I guess maybe the ten."

Jasper half laughed and half shouted, "You don't *know*? I thought you were psychic!"

"The cards have to be read in context," Faith started to raise her voice, as well. "The three of swords can imply infidelity, or divorce, or fertility problems, or just a bad day-"

"Well then, how do you choose?!"

"It depends on the person asking the questions!"

"So why didn't you give Kelsey the 'bad day' interpretation?!"

Faith slammed her hands down and leaned over the table, "Because, Jasper, she was clearly having an affair!"

Jasper sat back and his eyes went wide.

Faith gasped and threw a hand over her mouth. She could not believe what she had just blurted out, and she tried desperately to compose herself. It was as though Faye - the great and mysterious oracle - had swept into the room, divined the truth, and then abandoned the air just as swiftly, and she'd left Faith - the anxious and evicted klutz-next-door - screaming at the only customers her store had seen in a week.

A knock sounded at the door, and Charlotte poked her head around the frame. "Everything okay here, partner?" she asked carefully, giving Jasper the side eye. "My massage clients next door aren't exactly getting the relaxation they need, you know?"

"Yeah, sorry Charlie," Faith sat back down and dropped her volume, "please assure your customers that the Tarot cards can bring out the worst in us-"

"-but that they're always honest," Jasper added.

He reached across the table and put a hand over Faith's. She felt a heat slowly burn its way up her arm.

Charlotte gave them both one more glare, then closed the door again.

Faith briefly squeezed his hand back, then let go. She didn't want to feel anything more than she already did. This was not a relationship; it was a client interaction.

"Okay. Let's do this for real, then." Jasper collected the cards from the table.

Faith wasn't sure what he meant until he started shuffling.

He saw her watching him and offered the deck to her. "Are you supposed to do this?"

"You can if you want," she shrugged him off. "The cards will tell me what I need to know about you no matter whether you shuffle and deal them out or I do."

"They will, will they? Will they tell you everything about what's going through my head right now?" Jasper raised an eyebrow and tossed the cards between his hands like a professional poker player.

"They will absolutely tell me what's in your head, if I need to know it."

"And what if I grab one from the middle instead of the top?" he forced her to watch him gently ease his finger into the center of the deck and split it.

Faith bit her lip, imagining her body as the deck of cards. She looked straight into his eyes and whispered, "then in the middle of the deck is the card that wishes to present itself to you."

"It is, huh?" Jasper stopped caressing the inside of the deck and slammed it shut. "What if I change my mind last minute and grab the top one instead?"

He flicked the top card at her repeatedly until her face started to flush.

She pushed the feeling down. "Then that's the card that wishes to present itself to you, instead."

Jasper's tone changed from seductive to skeptical. "Well, I want both cards," he said.

"Greedy, aren't we? But go ahead," Faith licked her lips and leaned forward "pull both, and I'll read whatever is put in front of me."

Jasper threw two cards face up on the table, first from the center of the deck, and the next from the top. A third card slipped out from the middle and landed face down.

He went to retrieve it, but Faith reached for his hand to stop him.

A shock sparked between them again. She could tell he felt it too, and she didn't need to say anything more about it.

"The cards stay where they fall," she reprimanded him.

Jasper put the rest of the deck down, sat back, and folded his arms across his muscular chest.

Faith looked at the face-up cards.

"The Lovers," she read the first card and tried desperately to invoke Faye's stoic persona to keep herself from blushing. "The Lovers have been together since the beginning of time. This card tells me you'll bounce back from your relationship problems just fine."

Faith couldn't help herself from flirting, "that is, if you haven't bounced back already."

Jasper looked down at the card, but she wondered if he was doing so to try and hide the redness coloring on his cheeks.

He coughed, "and what are some of the other interpretations of this card, just so I'm prepared for anything."

Faith sat back and adapted from sexy to serious. "Ah, education time. Okay. Let's say you were thinking about starting a new business and you pulled the Lovers. I'd tell you that things would work out because what your head knows is perfectly aligned with what your heart wants."

Jasper chuckled, "is it now? Interesting."

"Sometimes it means you and a partner are at the same level."

"That certainly doesn't apply to me."

Faith continued, "Alternatively, it could mean that your life is in a lovely balance between sidewalk repairs and seal volunteering," Faith laughed, "that sort of thing."

"See? But that isn't fair," Jasper taunted, "because you know those two things about me already."

"I've figured out a ton about what is in your head, so much more than what you've told me, just by watching you fumble awkwardly with those cards," Faith insisted.

"Is that so?"

"It is."

They stared at each other for several seconds, and Faith questioned whether she should stay all business, or take a chance and be bold.

She reminded herself that she was being evicted from her apartment and would probably have to close the shop soon, which might mean moving far away from where she would ever see Jasper or anyone in the town again.

So, she went for it.

"First, judging by the way you teased me with my own cards, I know you're probably absolutely killer in bed."

Jasper made a sheepish face, but he continued to stare daggers into her soul. "That's an easy one, I obviously am. Tell me something else."

She'd seen the second card when he'd flipped them over, so she didn't need to take her eyes away from it. She stared into his eyes. "The Ten of Pentacles tells me you come from a legacy of people who know exactly what they want, and they go get it."

"That's obvious, you've met my Grandmother."

"Fine," Faith agreed reluctantly, "I have one more ace up my sleeve, as it were."

Jasper watched her closely as she flipped over the third card, the one that had jumped out unexpectedly when he was messing with the deck.

The reversed Page of Pentacles appeared.

For a moment, Faith had no idea what this represented, but slowly Faye's divining skills took over, and she felt the meaning come to her from deep within her stomach.

"The person Kelsey was having an affair with works for you."

Jasper stared into the card for a moment, then he started to scoff, "Pfft, she could have told you that-"

then he looked up at her in surprise and understanding. "But she didn't tell you that, because you didn't know she was-."

Faith started to say "Right, because I thought maybe you-"

"Wait! -because you thought *I* was the one having an affair?!" Jasper stood up and glared at the cards rather than Faith.

Faith held her breath. She hadn't gotten that part figured out when she did Kelsey's reading, yet she'd been correct about the affair itself. There had been an affair, but she hadn't trusted her gut enough to say which one of them was cheating.

"I only had what was presented to me," she stated.

She kept watching him as he looked at the cards and paced the room. She could see he was starting to believe in her skills and that a million questions were running through his mind.

"Well," Jasper continued to pace and waved his hands at the cards, "who is it? I'll fire him."

Faith paused, then broke out into laughter. She picked up the Lovers and the reversed Page.

"Don't bother. This guy-" she waved the reversed page back and forth, "-he is nothing, and he means nothing. He's a much smaller man than you-"

She saw a flash of humor cross Jasper's eyes and knew what he was thinking.

"Yes," she flirted, "I mean he's smaller in *every* way. Kelsey coming after him wasn't entirely his fault, either. She's stunning and manipulative, and he was weak."

Jasper smiled, "I bet it was Bill. He's such a dumbass."

Faith continued, "no matter who is was, you can leave the two of them to their own silly lives. The Lovers card tells me that you've still got the upper hand in love."

"I hope so," Jasper said, and looked from the cards to Faith.

She parted her lips.

Business Faye smacked her out of it and she broke the eye contact, putting extra effort to place the Page and Lovers back into the deck, and standing up to indicate that the reading was over.

"Well, there you go then," she said. "Good Tarot reading, I think."

"Tell me one more thing, about that card-" he pointed at the Ten of Pentacles which remained alone on the table.

Faith shrugged and moved to open the door for him. "Often the Ten implies an inheritance, but I certainly wouldn't wish for anyone you know to die-" her mind immediately went to Eleanor.

"-like Grandma? No way, she has more life left in her than I do," Jasper insisted.

Faith smiled, relieved.

As he entered the reception room, Jasper noted the aghast expressions on the other patrons.

He joked, "whew boy! Watch out folks, it gets heated in there!"

A few customers laughed, but Faith saw their eyes widen expectantly and excitedly, wondering what angry Faye might yell at *them* about.

Business-wise, Faye would do simply fine today.

CHAPTER SEVENTEEN

Sunday morning, Faith woke up and wanted to die. Every bone in her body ached. Saturday had been nonstop Tarot cards, Runes, palm readings, tea leaves, and one customer even asked for an extremely archaic phrenology - or head bump - reading. Faith had almost turned him down, but the fifty bucks he was offering was too good to pass up. She wasn't the world's best phrenologist, if any of them even existed anymore, but she felt in tune enough to understand what kinds of answers the guy was looking for. She figured he also desperately wanted a head massage.

It was exhilarating to have her abilities back, but damn if it didn't make her body feel two hundred years old the next day.

She all but crawled to the kitchen and turned on the coffee maker, and it took at least twenty seconds of listening to it whir to life before she realized she was still out of beans.

She smacked the machine in ire and stuck her slippers on. She'd limp to the coffee shop in her PJ pants to save herself from a morning without caffeine. Exhaustion did that to a person.

She was lucky, as most of the town would be at church, so there wasn't much risk of being seen by anyone who might *tut-tut* about her pajamas later. The busybodies would be occupied until well after noon, for sure.

On the way out of the apartment she noticed a court summons hanging on her mailbox, and she sighed. If an eviction court date was already booked, it meant she'd have a couple of weeks until the court visit, and then maybe a couple of weeks after that to get out, but it only gave her about a month to search for a new place.

After the previous day's steady business, she was feeling pretty good about income, but she didn't know how she'd be able to gather enough for first and last month's rent on a new place.

"I suppose I *will* have to live at the shop," she said to herself as she walked out of the building and crossed the road. "Charlie's massage table would make a great bed."

"You dare sleep on my table, and you'll be cleaning it every damn hour," Charlotte's voice boomed from somewhere.

Faith spun around in circles to see where it was coming from, and she tripped over her slippers.

Charlie laughed, and Faith spotted her on Eleanor's front porch.

"No cute boy to save your clumsy ass this time, Faye-Faye," Charlie chuckled, walking down the steps to help her up.

Faith waved her off and stood up on her own, clutching her sore back as she did so. She groaned.

"I hear that," Charlie said, "yesterday was a nightmare."

"An amazing nightmare, though."

"Come on up, Eleanor is making tea for all of us."

"How'd you know I'd come out here?"

"Babe, I know you. You've been out of coffee for a week and there was no way you remembered to stop for it on the way home last night. For a magical and mysterious psychic, you are as predictable as all get out." Charlie punched her in the arm and added "plus, I saw the eviction notice. You'd be forced out eventually."

Faith crossed her arms in a huff. She walked up the short steps and noticed that the lovely wicker furnishings had been replaced with camping chairs. Disappointed, she chose one that faced her ugly townhouse apartment, so she could convince herself that being evicted was the best thing for her.

The camping chairs looked to be in worse shape than her living situation, and yet when she sat down she felt consumed with welcome, like sitting on a cloud.

The work yesterday must have really done a number on me, she thought.

Eleanor approached the screen door carrying a large tray of tea and cookies. Charlie popped up to open the door and help her with it.

"These chairs aren't the prettiest," said Eleanor, "but my kids have taken almost everything else now. The last thing left to go is me!"

Charlie started, "I'm sorry, Mrs.-"

"Eleanor, and don't worry about it. I'm looking forward to seeing what JJ does with this place."

Faith nearly dropped her tea, "JJ? You mean Jasper?"

"Yes," Eleanor beamed. "Turns out I'm a little more than bitter that my kids forced me out at such a young age-"

She paused to haughtily primp her silver hair.

Charlie snickered, "You tell 'em!"

"-so, I made the executive decision to leave the house to JJ. I told him last night."

"The Ten of Pentacles," Faith whispered. Her gift was back.

"There's another thing," Eleanor added, handing a cookie to Faith. "Since he lives in the City, I said I wanted him to rent it out to you."

Faith nearly dropped her cookie. "Oh Eleanor, I couldn't possibly-"

"-but you must," Eleanor insisted. "You're the only one who noticed and appreciated the fairy garden, the meditation altar my love built for me, and everything else I've curated over the years to create this sacred space. My kids thought it was all junk, and now whatever I didn't manage to save for your shop is all either sold or traded back and forth between them, but-"

"-the feeling is still here," Charlie said, settling deeper into her camping chair.

Faith felt it, too, the magic of this little cottage in Fallstaff, Missouri.

However, her practical, businesslike brain took over and she couldn't help but wonder about the specifics. "Do you think Jasper will mind?"

"Why don't you ask him yourself," Eleanor said, and nodded to his car quietly pulling up to the curb.

CHAPTER EIGHTEEN

Eleanor turned to Charlie, "there are a couple of things still upstairs I'd like to give the shop. I thought they might be nice for your massage studio."

Charlie didn't need a second request to leave Faith and Jasper alone. She stood and opened the screen door, and the two women disappeared into the house.

"Hey," Jasper said, rounding the front of his car.

"Hey," Faith replied.

"Did my Gran talk to you about ?"

"-yeah. It's so nice of her but listen, I don't want this to get weird," Faith said honestly.

"It's definitely weird," Jasper agreed, then he waved a finger between them, "but whatever is happening here is very weird, as well."

"Oh yeah?" Faith raised an eyebrow and waved her finger between them, too, "Just what do you think is happening here?"

Jasper looked away and shuffled his feet, "you tell me, you're the psychic."

"I can't do predictions for myself," Faith grinned and stood up, "I know too much insider info about me."

"Then let me try," Jasper said, holding out a hand.

She put her palm in his, and the same small electric shock that had flashed between them so many times before sparked again.

Jasper chuckled and looked at her palm. He scratched his bottom lip, pretending to be in deep thought over the meaning of the lines and ridges crossing her hand.

Faith laughed, "you have no idea what you're looking at, do you?"

"Of course I do," he lied. "I see you living in my Grandmother's house-"

"-your house-"

"-My *grandmother's* house," Jasper reiterated, "she's still got plenty of life left in her. I'll just be taking care of the upkeep."

"Like a landlord does," Faith shook her head.

"Like a *grandson* does," Jasper poked her in the hand and pretended to read her life line. "Anyway, you'll pay rent to *her*, which will help out with the cost of moving her to a bigger suite at the retirement community."

"She did want to be near the water," Faith agreed.

"And you need to be near your shop," Jasper smiled. He held her hand up to show it to her. "Does that all sound correct?"

Faith laughed, but she looked at her palm. It was if the warmth of his touch had added depth to her heart line.

She closed her hand and took it back, self-conscious. "Yeah, that sounds pretty spot on."

"Great." Now it was Jasper's turn to adjust himself self-consciously. "Okay, so I have to get over to the zoo. Before I go, did you want me to trim back the rest of the clematis on the sidewalk?"

"Not today, Mr. Landlord-"

"*Landlord's grandson,*" Jasper interjected, "I'm not getting into that game, remember?"

"-the fairy garden overgrowth has brought me nothing but good luck this year," Faith smiled into his eyes, and their Tiger's Eye hue brought her back to that day on the sidewalk.

Before she could look away, he leaned in and kissed her. She almost stumbled backwards over the steps, but he caught her in his arms, his lips still planted on hers.

She kissed him back, and it felt as if their lips had been together since the beginning of time.

"The Lovers card," she whispered when he finally let go.

"That was my favorite part of the reading."

"Mine too," she replied.

Charlie emerged from the house, either completely unaware of what was happening, or doing a fairly good job of hiding it. She held sheets in her arms. "Look Faye, Egyptian cotton!"

Faith laughed, "that's awesome. Want to bring them to the store now?"

Charlie winked, "I'll bring them over there and start setting up the displays with those boxes from yesterday. Why don't you take the day off?"

Faith started to protest, but Charlie persisted, "I'm no magical oracle, but I can read Tarot cards if any customer comes in. You two should probably finish what you started there."

Charlie *did* know what was happening between Faith and Jasper.

Faith blushed.

"I think that's a lovely idea," agreed Eleanor, coming out of the cottage. "I'll help Charlotte, too. It will give me something to do before my kids come and drag me away from this town. You two go finish smooching at the zoo."

So Eleanor knew they'd kissed, too. Now it was Jasper's turn to blush.

"I'd love to see the zoo," Faith told him.

"Are you sure? Cleaning seal pens is not a great first date."

Faith laughed, "neither is tripping over a hedge and throwing rocks all over the place, but it seemed to work out for me."

"I never did get that jasper you promised me."

"Oops, did I promise you a Jasper as well?" She teased, "because I certainly found one for myself."

THE END

About the Author

Emmy Tidning lives in a magical fantasy world called the Pacific Northwest, where anything is possible but no one is real. She has two cats, a dog, a husband, some kids, and a widowed crow she befriended using peanuts. Emmy reads Tarot cards, writes clean romantic fun, and can be reached through the publisher at info@applieddivination.com

Acknowledgments

This book would not exist without:
1) Fortune teller insight from Emily Paper at Applied Divination.
2) Paranormal women's fiction writing tips, and tons of Zoom conference calls, with author TJ Deschamps. Check out her Faerie Tales series on Amazon!
3) Encouragement from the Romance Writing community, the Cascade Writers nonprofit organization, and the Speculative Twist Facebook group.
4) The love and support of my husband, Hoover.

Also Published by Applied Divination

Applied Tarot
Applied Runes
Psychic Word Puzzles
Charlie's Chill

Visit emilypaper.com for more information.

Applied Tarot
REVERSED

An Excessively Practical Guide to Interpreting Reversed Tarot Cards

What movie should you watch when you pull
The Hermit reversed?

The Hermit

XI

You should watch **The Truman Show!**

I will never stop recommending the Truman Show.
When you watch it this time, pay attention to extra
details you may have missed- the travel agent who
arrives with a makeup bib on. The friend who "got
pneumonia" probably as an excuse for a work
vacation.
The Truman Show is fascinating. So are reversed
Tarot Cards!

**Follow emilypaper.com for more
information**

Coming Soon from Emmy Tidning

Charlie's Chill

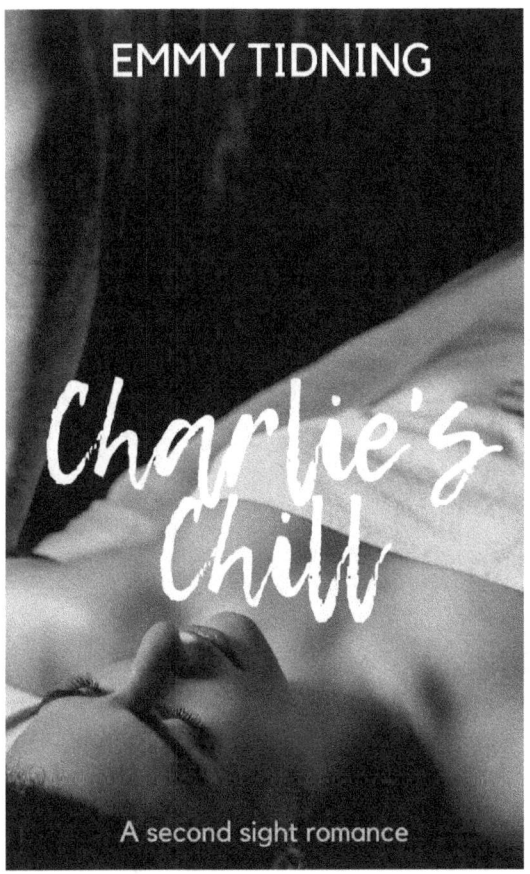

EMMY TIDNING

Charlie's Chill

A second sight romance

For a smooth-talking, tranquility-touting Reiki massage therapist, Charlotte is anything but calm. Her business is barely scraping by, her partner is love-struck, her friend is paranoid, and she's somehow always in two places at once. Can a truck driver's son talk her down off the ledge, or has he got her all stressed out, too?

Chill out with Charlotte in *Charlie's Chill*, summer 2021

www.ingramcontent.com/pod-product-compliance
Lightning Source LLC
Chambersburg PA
CBHW051924220626
47052CB00003B/565